A DAY AT THE SEASIDE

by James Driscoll
Illustrated by Rob Lee

Storm Publishing

It was a beautiful day. The sun was shining so brightly that it seemed to be smiling. The sea was very calm. The water was so clear that you could see the golden sand below. There were lots of fish swimming in and out of the rocks and seaweed. This was a perfect day for a trip to the seaside.

The sound of a loud voice echoed across the beach, "LEFT, RIGHT, LEFT, RIGHT, HA---LT! Put everything down here." The Shoe People had arrived. Everybody recognised that military voice. Yes, of course, it was Sergeant Major.

"Really Sergeant Major, there is no need to shout, we can all hear perfectly well, we are not deaf," said Trampy. Then he turned to the others and told them to unpack their bags.

Charlie was so excited that he started to gambol over and over in the lovely soft sand. He was going so quickly that he forgot to look where the water met the sand and suddenly, to his surprise, there was a loud SPLASH! Charlie was a very wet clown.

Flip-Flop and Baby Bootee laughed and laughed. They thought that Charlie was the funniest clown in the whole world.

"Stupid clown!," said Sergeant Major looking at Charlie in disgust. "Two years in the Army would do you good, make a man of you, teach you to be responsible."

"Sergeant Major, we have come to the seaside to enjoy ourselves," said Trampy. "And we do not want to listen to lectures from you all day. Go and march up and down the beach, you always feel better after a long march."

"Very well, I do not need telling twice," said Sergeant Major and he marched off muttering to himself.

Flip-Flop had decided that she was going to sunbathe on the rocks.

"Please be careful Flip-Flop, the tide is coming in and if a strong wave breaks over the rocks it could just wash you into the sea," said Trampy.

Baby Bootee was building sand castles. She was collecting sea shells from the water's edge and putting them on top of the sand castles, making beautiful patterns. What a lovely time she was having crawling very quickly out of the way of the waves as they ran along the sand towards her.

Trampy was sitting on the beach reading one of his favourite nature books but keeping a watchful eye on them all.

Charlie, who had now dried out, decided that the time had come for some fun and games. He began to pull silly faces. He then started to squirt them all with water from the daisy on the top of his hat.

Sergeant Major was still marching up and down the beach. He had reached the rocks where Flip-Flop had gone to sunbathe.

Suddenly a voice cried out,
"Help! Help! Somebody help me quickly!"

Sergeant Major climbed on to the rocks as fast as he could and, sure enough, there in the sea was poor Flip-Flop. The very thing that Trampy had warned her about had happened. She had fallen asleep in the sunshine and a wave had washed over the rocks, sweeping her into the sea.

Sergeant Major shouted in his loudest army voice, "Trampy, Charlie, look sharp, over here, on the double! Flip-Flop has fallen off the rocks into the sea!"

Trampy and Charlie raced to the rocks.
"Please do something, I seem to be floating further out to sea," cried Flip-Flop.

"Don't panic Flip-Flop," said Trampy, "we will soon have you out of the water. Charlie, your lace is very long, hurry, take it out of your shoe."

Charlie began to take out the lace as fast as he could. It seemed to take such a long time because he had so many lace holes to pull it through. Finally it was out.

"There you are Trampy," said Charlie as he passed him the lace.

"Flip-Flop I am going to throw one end of Charlie's lace towards you, grab hold of it tightly and we will pull you to the rocks," said Trampy. "Sergeant Major you get as close as you can to the water and when Flip-Flop gets near the rocks help her onto them."

Trampy swung the lace over his head twice and then threw one end to Flip-Flop.

"I've got it Trampy," she shouted.

"Are you ready Charlie?" asked Trampy. Charlie nodded. They both pulled and pulled on the lace and slowly but surely Flip-Flop reached the rock where Sergeant Major stood. He stretched out to her and was able to catch hold of her hand and help her from the sea. Flip-Flop was very happy to be back with her friends again.

"You are truly the best friends that anyone could ever have, you have saved my life," said Flip-Flop, very relieved.

Charlie was so pleased that Flip-Flop had been saved with HIS lace that he somersaulted off the rocks on to the beach squirting water from the daisy on his hat, hitting Sergeant Major.

They all laughed. Well almost all of them.

There was just one comment from Sergeant Major. Can you guess what he said?
That's right.

"STUPID CLOWN!".